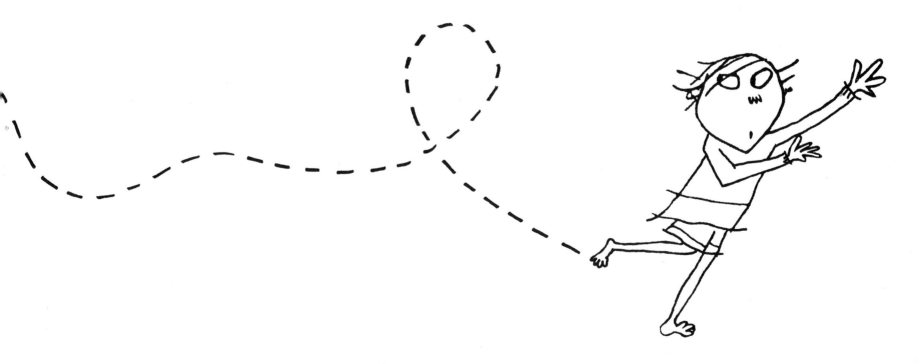

My Uncle is a hunkle.

He says things like **Gotcha Baby**

and

Eat dirt ding bat.

He watches too many films.

He's a fireman so he wears special trousers. He's always rescuing people from tall toppling buildings which are going up in a cloud of smoke.

He can have you in a fireman's lift
before you can say

Uncle Ted put me down!

He says
he has had
plenty of close shaves
which is funny
because he has a beard.
Mum says me and
Uncle Ted get on
like a house on fire.

This book is for my
sister Rachel, who was
crazy about guinea pigs
and for my sister Jenny,
who preferred cars.

RACHEL

JENNY

♡
also for
my friend
Lindsay
Isobel
Hart

Thanks
to Olga
at the
guinea
pig
rescue
centre

ORCHARD BOOKS
338 Euston Road, London NW1 3BH

Orchard Books Australia
Hachette Children's Books
Level 17/207 Kent Street, Sydney, NSW 2000

ISBN 1 84121 399 3 (hardback)
ISBN 1 84121 624 0 (paperback)

First published in Great Britain in 2000
First paperback publication in 2001

© Lauren Child 2000

The right of Lauren Child to be identified
as the author and the illustrator of this
work has been asserted by her
in accordance with the Copyright,
Designs and Patents Act, 1988.

Designed by
Anna-Louise Billson

A CIP catalogue record for this book
is available from the British Library.

2 3 4 5 6 7 8 9 10 (hardback)
10 (paperback)

Printed in Singapore

My Uncle is a Hunkle
says Clarice Bean

ORCHARD BOOKS

We got a phone call
at quarter past five
in the morning.

It turned out Uncle Ernie *slipped* on a doughnut
getting out of his squad car.

He's a
policeman in
New York City
so he's used
to life's
ups and *downs*.

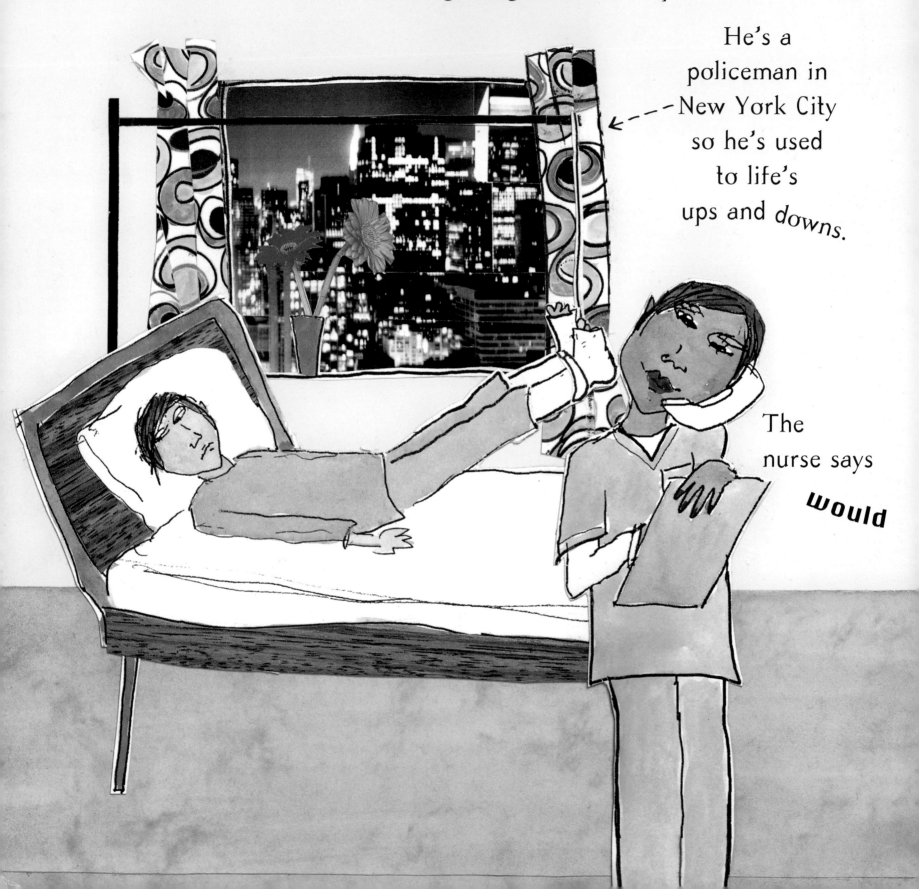

The
nurse says

would

Mum nip out there on the double because he's lying flat on his back with both legs in the air.

Mum says,

What was he thinking of eating doughnuts at a time like this anyway?

But of course she has to go.

Someone will have to babysit because
Dad is also about to go away on Important Business.

Marcie (my big sister) says,
**I would rather look after newts
from Neptune than
be left with Clarice Bean** (me)
and Minal Cricket
(my little brother).

Kurt
(my big brother)
says,

**Don't look at me, I'm going
to my room and probably
won't be down for supper.**

Minal says,

What
about
Grandad?

Grandad says,
I haven't had
a doughnut
since I was
a boy.

Mum rings round all her friends for a babysitter.
Then she rings round all her
friends' friends
but everybody says
they are busy.

Dad says,

Who can
blame them?

I'll be with you
in two shakes,
Bernard.

I say,

How about
Uncle
Ted?

Mum goes a bit pale.

Uncle Ted is Mum's younger brother.

When Uncle Ted fancies a break from fire fighting
and cats up trees he comes round to our house.
Whenever he's
around it gets really noisy.

Get off your horse
and drink your milk.

Uncle Ted and I love to watch westerns on the edge of our seats
with a plate of egg and beans
perched on our laps.

Uncle Ted is teaching me cowboy techniques.
Last week he lassoed the lamp.

Mum said,
I'd rather have everything in one piece
thank you very much.

Uncle Ted looked sheepish.
I lassoed my brother.
He wasn't too happy either.

So you can see why Mum is nervous about leaving Uncle Ted in charge but it turns out she can't be so choosy. Mum gives Uncle Ted some **very** strict instructions.

1. NO BREAKAGES

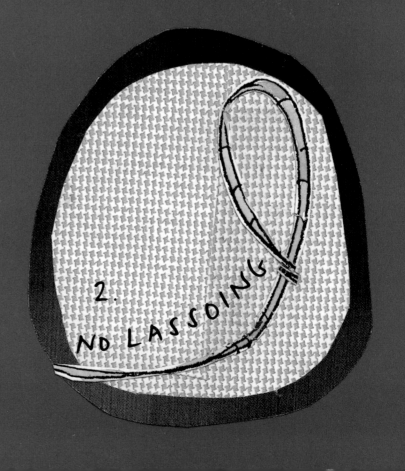

2. NO LASSOING

3. DON'T DRIVE MRS STAMPNEY AT NUMBER 9 DOO-LALLY

4. MAKE SURE KURT SEES THE DAYLIGHT AT LEAST ONCE EVERY 24 HOURS

5. DON'T LET MARCIE TAKE THE PHONE INTO HER BEDROOM

chat chat chat chat chat chat chat chat chat

6. KEEP AN EYE ON GRANDAD HE TENDS TO WANDER OFF

Uncle Ted says,

Yes Maam. I hear you loud and clear.

Everything goes **really well** for the first two days.

Nobody is arguing and we are like one of those families on your television who always say things like

please

and

thank you

and

sorry . . .

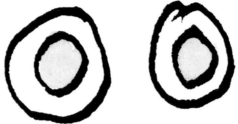

...and they let people share their things without grumbling.

Kurt even sits in the garden and almost nearly gets a tan. He never normally goes outside, he says it's too bright.

BUT THEN . . .

Minal ruins everything
by getting Albert out of his hutch without asking.
I am the one looking after him for the holidays.
(Albert is the school guinea pig so it's a VERY
RESPONSIBLE
JOB.)

Albert

Albert makes

I am beside myself because I **know** he will never be seen again.

Minal and I are racing round the kitchen table. Minal is squealing and I am trying to flip his nose with a carrot.

a dash for it.

Lots
of
things
get
broken.

Drop the carrot, little lady.

Luckily for Minal Cricket,
Uncle Ted comes in to rescue him.

To take my mind
off the worry of
losing a guinea pig
we all go outside
    and play football.
And it works because

Uncle Ted kicks the ball so hard that it knocks Minal out.

We have to **drive** to the emergency room at **50** miles an hour at least!

Hang on to your trousers.

Minal is fine but they give him an X-ray and a little carton of orange juice.

Minal loves it because he can show off and lie under a blanket whimpering.

I say he should have stitches but unfortunately the nurse doesn't agree.

When we get home we find Grandad is missing.
Uncle Ted phones round all the neighbours
and is about to dial 999 when
Mrs Stampney at Number 9
calls to say she has found Grandad
sitting
in
her
sitting room.

Watching the racing.

She's quite grumpy about it.

Uncle Ted says,

How in tarnation did you end up here?

Grandad says,
    All the houses look the same,
it's a job to tell them apart without my glasses.

    But I know it's really because
Mrs Stampney's got a bigger television set than us
        and it's got a remote control.

I'm still worried to pieces about Albert so I go into the garden
to see if he has come back to his hutch.

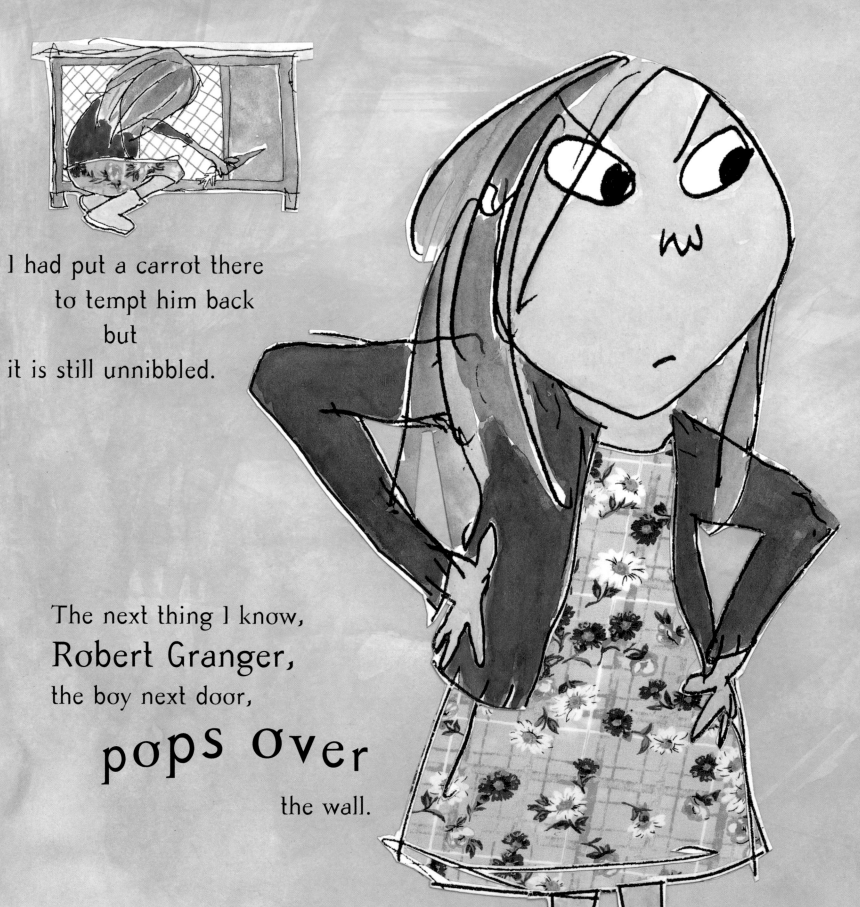

I had put a carrot there
to tempt him back
but
it is still unnibbled.

The next thing I know,
Robert Granger,
the boy next door,

pops over

the wall.

He says,

Do you want to stroke my guinea pig?

I say, That's not your guinea pig that's Albert.

He says,

It's not Albert she's Belinda.

I say,

You better give him back Robert Granger that's School Property and you will be in big trouble with the Police.

Robert Granger is so nervous he lets Albert wriggle out of his hands.

Albert is s c u t t l i n g through the house

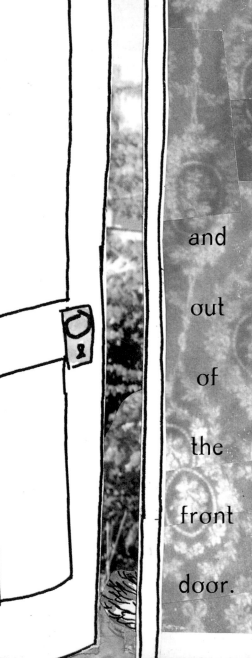

and out of the front door.

Uncle Ted shouts,

After him.

We are madly c h a s i n g the loose guinea pig who is charging through the railings.

Minal squeezes past him and gets **wedged** like a giant squeaking tomato.
I say, Lucky you are here Uncle Ted because you will have him rescued in next to no time.

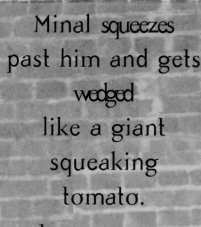

(Rescuing people from railings is normal for Uncle Ted and he doesn't look a bit bothered.)

Uncle Ted says, **Hang in there Buddy,**

and he shoots off to call his friends at the fire station. But it takes him ages to find the phone.

chat
chat
chat
chat
. . . so anyway, I said . . .
chat chat
chat
. . . and then guess what he said . . .

chat
chat
chat
chat
chat

In the meantime,
Mum arrives back from the airport.
She delves straight in her bag
for her new bottle of bubble bath
and rubs it on Minal's head.
She squidges him out in almost
less than two
minutes.

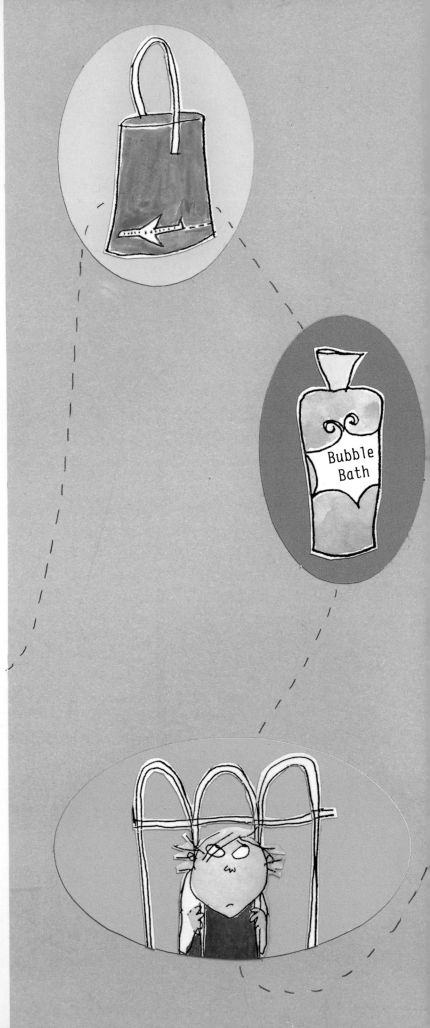

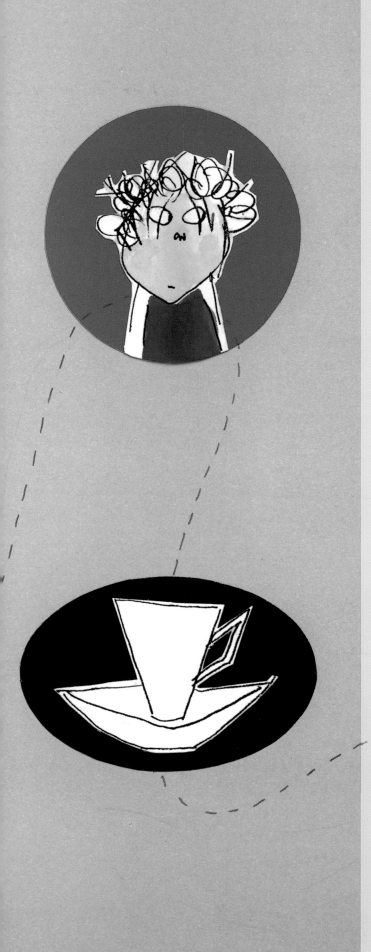

She says, *I wouldn't mind a quiet cup of tea in the garden.*

But then guess what happens?

Nearly all the whole
fire brigade turns up.
Mum doesn't
even look one bit
surprised.
She just looks at
Uncle Ted.

Minal,
already rescued

Uncle Ted says,
**Don't blame
me, blame that
guinea pig,
Albert.**

Belinda!

It turns out Uncle Ernie is feeling quite chirpy now but he doesn't think he will ever be able to look at a doughnut again.

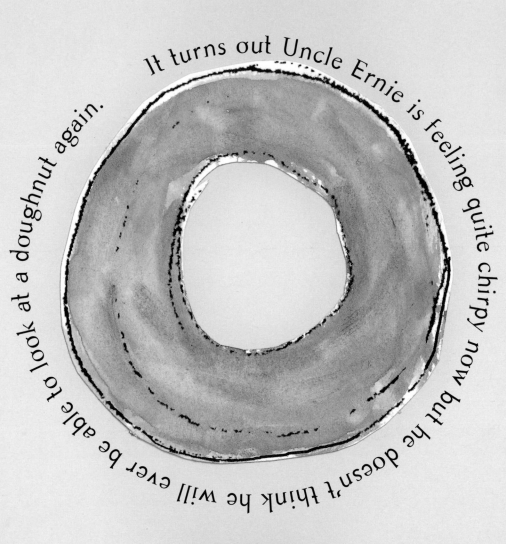

He says,

Mine's a **double cheeseburger** with **fries** and a **banana milkshake** to go.

And as for Uncle Ted, he says,
Babysitting is the hardest job I've ever done.

I say,
Harder than firefighting?
Uncle Ted says,
You better believe it baby.

Albert, finally found
9½ hours later

My Uncle is a hunkle.

Mum says we get on like a house on fire.

This Faber book belongs to

Read the book, sing the song,
watch the film, dance along!
kitchendiscobook.com

KT-415-826

For the beloved Foges fruit –
Mum, Chris, Barley, Harry and Molly
C. F.

To Kim, Dave & Gareth –
my own Kitchen Disco crew
A. M.

'THIS IS SO FUNNY, DOES THIS
REALLY HAPPEN WHEN I GO TO BED?'
JOSH, AGE 5

FABER & FABER has published children's books since 1929. Some of our very first publications included *Old Possum's Book of Practical Cats* by T. S. Eliot, starring the now world-famous Macavity, and *The Iron Man* by Ted Hughes. Our catalogue at the time said that 'it is by reading such books that children learn the difference between the shoddy and the genuine'. We still believe in the power of reading to transform children's lives.

First published in the UK in 2015, and first published in the USA in 2017, by Faber and Faber Limited, Bloomsbury House, 74–77 Great Russell Street, London WC1B 3DA.
Text copyright © Clare Foges, 2015. Illustration copyright © Al Murphy, 2015. ISBN 978-0-571-30788-3 All rights reserved. Printed in India.

9 10

The moral rights of Clare Foges and Al Murphy have been asserted. A CIP record for this book is available from the British Library.

MIX
Paper from
responsible sources
FSC® C016779
www.fsc.org

KITCHEN DISCO

↠ A FABER PICTURE BOOK ↞

WRITTEN BY
CLARE FOGES

ILLUSTRATED BY
AL MURPHY

BANANARAMA

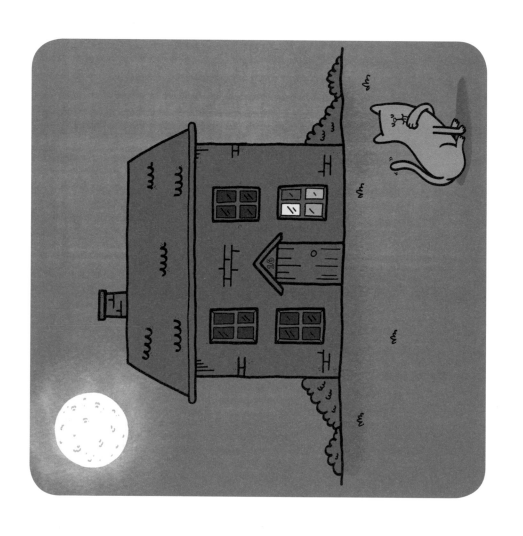

AT NIGHT WHEN YOU ARE SLEEPING
THERE'S A PARTY IN YOUR HOUSE.

IT'S A PUMPING, JUMPING, FUNKY BASH WHEN ALL THE LIGHTS GO OUT...

IN THE QUIET OF YOUR KITCHEN

WHEN THE MOON IS SHINING WHITE

THE FRUIT JUMP FROM THE FRUIT BOWL
AND THEY DANCE ALL THROUGH THE NIGHT!

HE SOMERSAULTS,

HE SPINS,

HE JUMPS,

THEN DOES BANANA SPLITS.

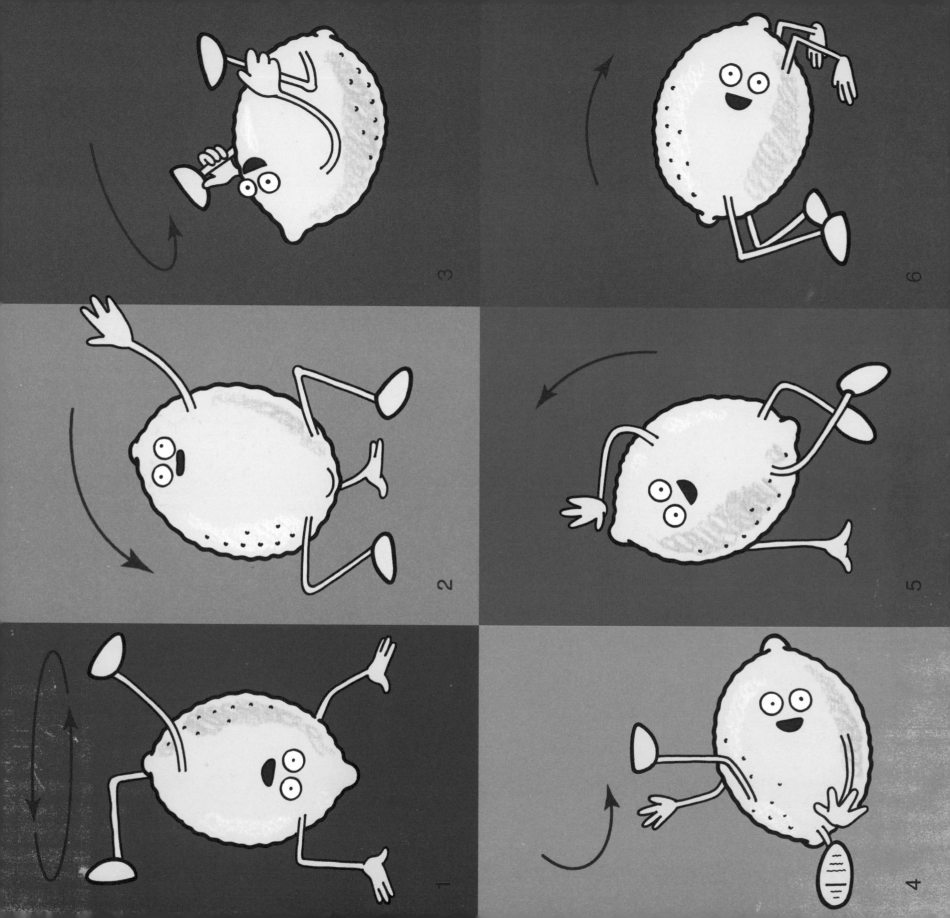

THE **LEMONS** ARE
THE SHOW-OFFS
THEY REALLY LOVE TO RAP
THEY BREAK DANCE ON THE
CHOPPING BOARD
AND TAP DANCE ON THE TAP...

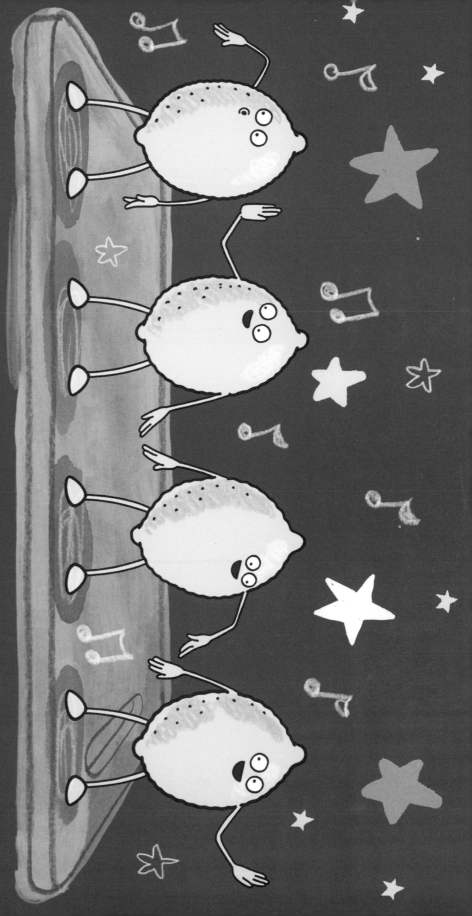

THE COCONUT
IS CHEEKY, HE MAKES
THE OTHERS LAUGH,

HE DIVES INTO THE WASHING-UP...
AND HAS A BUBBLE BATH!

SO SHAKE IT LIKE A MANGO

PARTY LIKE A PEAR

WIGGLE LIKE AN APPLE,

HEY!

AND DANCE LIKE YOU DON'T CARE.

STRAWBERRIES RULE

IT'S CALLED THE
KITCHEN DISCO
AND EVERYONE'S INVITED
SO MOVE YOUR HIPS
SHAKE YOUR PIPS
AND LET'S GET ALL EXCITED!

TANGERINES

THE **TANGERINES**
Go BOUNCY-BOUNCE

THEY LIKE TO SCREAM AND SHOUT...

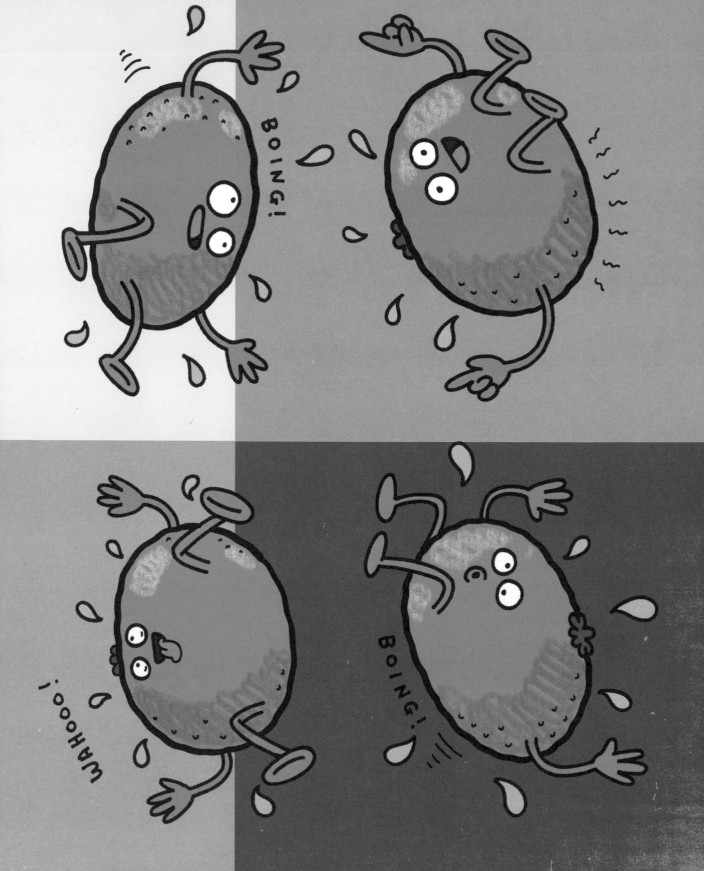

ONE TANGERINE SPUN
ROUND SO MUCH
THAT ALL HER JUICE CAME OUT!

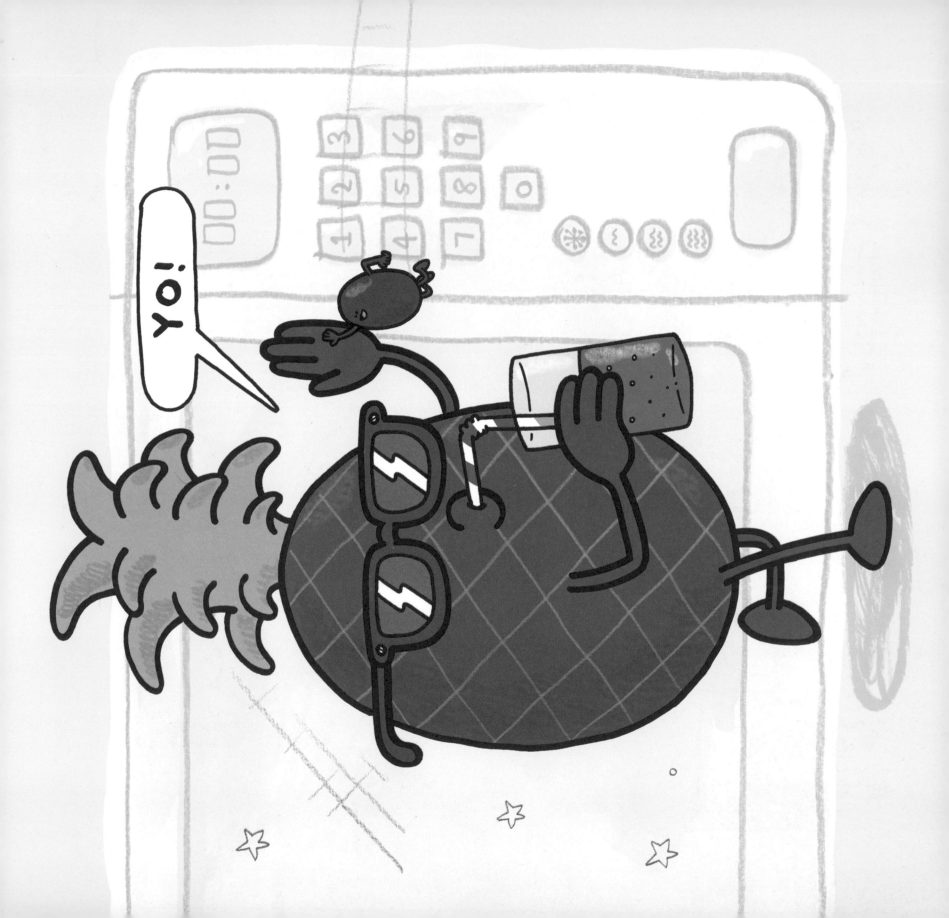

THE PINEAPPLE

IS VERY COOL

HE WEARS HIS HAIR IN SPIKES

HE HANGS OUT BY THE MICROWAVE

HIGH-FIVING FRUIT HE LIKES...

BA-DOING!

I ♥ PINEAPPLE!

So SHAKE IT LIKE A MANGO

PARTY LIKE A PEAR

WIGGLE LIKE AN APPLE,

HEY!

AND DANCE LIKE YOU DON'T CARE.

I ♥ APPLES

IT'S CALLED THE
KITCHEN DISCO
AND EVERYONE'S INVITED
SO MOVE YOUR HIPS
SHAKE YOUR PIPS
AND LET'S GET ALL EXCITED!

VERY BERRY

THE **GRAPES** ARE SUCH A SILLY BUNCH, THEY BOOGIE IN A CONGA! WHEN ALL THE OTHER FRUIT JOIN IN THE CONGA LINE GETS LONGER!

CONGA!

THE **PEARS**
HAVE BIG FAT
BOTTOMS,
THEY GROOVE
ACROSS THE
FLOOR...

THE **APPLES**
WAVE THEIR
STALKS AROUND
AND SCREAM
FOR
MORE
MORE
MORE!

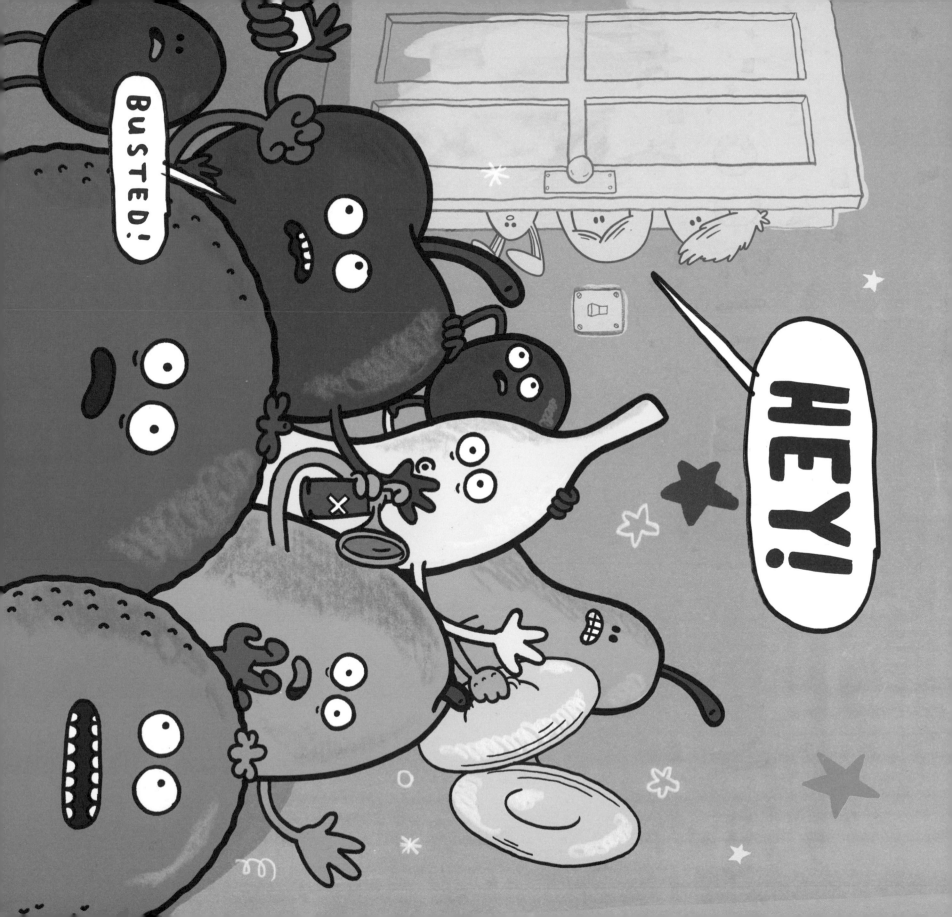

JUST DANCE LIKE YOU DON'T CARE! IT'S CALLED THE KITCHEN DISCO

AT BREAKFAST TIME, THE PARTY SLOWS.
THE FRUIT MUST GO TO BED.

THEY CLIMB IN TO THE FRUIT BOWL...
AND THEY REST THEIR SLEEPY HEADS.

So if You're in the Kitchen

And You Hear them them Sing this Song

Then Don't ask Why

And Don't be Shy –

Come on and Sing Along!